THE FAT-CATS AT SEA

by J. Patrick Lewis • illustrated by Victoria Chess

An Apple Soup Book

An Imprint of Alfred A. Knopf • New York

For Joanna Lewis Cole — J. P. L.

For Blair and Sandra with love — V. C.

Thanks to Myra Cohn Livingston, who first published a slightly
altered version of "An Octopus He and She" in *Valentine Poems*
(Holiday House, 1987).

APPLE SOUP IS A TRADEMARK OF ALFRED A. KNOPF, INC.

Text copyright © 1994 by J. Patrick Lewis
Illustrations copyright © 1994 by Victoria Chess

All rights reserved under International and Pan-American Copyright Conventions. Published in the United
States of America by Alfred A. Knopf, Inc., New York, and simultaneously in Canada by Random House
of Canada Limited, Toronto. Distributed by Random House, Inc., New York.
Book design by Edward Miller.

Library of Congress Cataloging-in-Publication Data

Lewis, J. Patrick.
The fat-cats at sea / by J. Patrick Lewis ; illustrated by Victoria Chess.
p.   cm.
"An Apple Soup Book"
Summary: At the command of the Queen of Catmandoo, the crew of cats aboard "The Frisky Dog" set sail
to find sticky-goo buns in this narrative verse.
ISBN 0-679-82639-4 (trade) — ISBN 0-679-92639-9 (lib. bdg.)
[1. Cats—Fiction. 2. Ships—Fiction. 3. Stories in rhyme.]   I. Title.
PZ8.3.L87 Fat   1994   91-31296   [E]—dc20

Manufactured in Singapore
10 9 8 7 6 5 4 3 2 1

CONTENTS

EXTRA! EXTRA! *The Midnight Cat*   8

The Voyage of *The Frisky Dog*   10

Hillary Hollery Q. McQatt Introduces the Crew   12

Stuck on the Equator   16

The Homesick Song of Rotten Stew   18

Lookout Louie in the Crow's Nest   20

Sticky-Goo at Last!   22

Attack on the Poodles   24

An Octopus He and She   26

On the Nowhere Isles   28

The First Mate and the Whale Islands   32

The Return of *The Frisky Dog*   34

EXTRA! EXTRA!
The Midnight Cat

Angoras, Persians, Calicos!
Tabbys, Toms, and Siamese!—
Or any Alley Cat who's ever
Sailed the seven seas!

Her Royal Highness calls upon
Courageous Cats like you,
Because there's not one Sticky-Bun
In all of Catmandoo!

Those Buns grow wild in Sticky-Goo
Upon a distant shore—
There's Catnip for the Sailors who
Can bring me back some more!

Somewhere over the navy blue,
Somewhere over the wavy green,

                  rising—

           rising,

Buns are rising,
Biggest Buns you've ever seen!

Bring 'em home, you Buccaneers!
Not petits fours, not elephant ears,
Just tons of Buns of Sticky-Goo!

      By Order of Her Majesty,

The Queen of Catmandoo

The Voyage of
The Frisky Dog

A dandy Manx from Captain's ranks
Addressed the village green,
"My ship, *The Frisky Dog*, will fly
The colors of the Queen!

"I'm off to find a tasty pastry
Fortune!" he meowed.
"Who else among you mousers wants
To make Her Highness proud?"

Behind him five fat felines bravely
Tiptoed up the board.
Saluting to the Palace Guard,
Each bravely raised a sword.

"We'll ride the winds that whip the waves,
And waves that rip the tide,
Until we find the pile of dough
With Sticky-Goo inside!"

And so begins a Fat-Cat tale,
Kept in the Captain's log,
Of Sticky-Buns and Buccaneers—
The tale of *The Frisky Dog*.

Hillary Hollery Q. McQatt
Introduces the Crew

I'm Hillary-dillery,
Hollery-dollery,
Hillary Hollery over the sea!
A potbellied cat,
Delightfully fat,
There's no one as tubby as me!

Yes, I'm the happy Captain Captain
H. H. Q. McQ.
And these are the adventures
Of my famous Fat-Cat crew!

The First Mate, Razor-Toes Jerome,
Deserves a name that draws
Attention to the rows of cactus
Needles on his paws.

The Cook is Stewart Rottenham,
Alias Rotten Stew,
Who makes a dish that's perfectly
Impossible to chew.

The Compass-Cat's in a bunk below,
Buried under maps,
Coloring them with crayons
When he isn't taking naps.

Lookout Lou writes Post-it notes
Upon a frying pan
And drops 'em down by yo-yo
To the Gunner, Catty Moran,

Who fires catnip cannonballs
Into the midnight sun,
So Lookout Louie can shout, "Gadzooey!"
As he catches 'em one by one.

Fat-Cats are long on kindness,
Fat-Cats are seldom rude,
Fat-Cats are known from coast to coast
For Fat-Cat gratitude.

Six furry Fat-Cat comrades,
Six favorite Fat-Cat sons!
We're off to fill—
We will, we will!—
One boatload full of Buns!

Stuck on the Equator

Now *The Frisky Dog* depended
For directions on a splendid
   Navigator, Compass-Cat.
Pushing buttons on his dials,
Or by pawing through his files,
He could navigate the miles
   To the Buns in nothing flat!

But the sound of distant thunder
Found Ol' Compass hiding under-
   neath the blankets on his bed.
It was several hours later
When that dizzy Navigator
Crossed the line at the equator—
   "It's a bungee cord!" he said.

"Captain Captain," cried the pouncer,
"I'm afraid I let you down, sir—
   For I lost my gyroscope!
When the weather gets this soggy,
All my instruments get foggy,
Which is why *The Frisky Doggy*
   Has collided with a rope!"

Oh, we might have bobbed forever
If it hadn't been for clever
   Razor-Toes Jerome, who cried:
"Hold her nice and steady, Skipper!"
Then he snapped it up to snip 'er
With his razor-toenail clipper,
   And we sailed off with the tide.

The Homesick Song
of Rotten Stew

On the Sea of the Goodgollygum
I'm so sad when I think of me Mum.
   So I send her a postcard
   Delivered by Coast Guard
Up the alley where I come from.

On the Sea of the Goodgollygee
I remember that one recipe
   I'd almost forgotten—
   Potatoes au gRotten!—
Me Mum used to bake for me.

On the Sea of the Goodgollygoon
There's a Cheshire cat grin on the moon
   That reminds me of some
   Silly grin on me Mum
Blown up like a big balloon.

Chorus

Goodgollygee and Goodgollygum,
Oh, golly, how I miss Goodgollymum!
It's awful for me,
Oh, how awful for Mum
On Calico Alley where I come from.
I'm farther than ever I wanted to be,
Under the stars on the Goodgolly Sea!

Lookout Louie in the Crow's Nest

Last to bed,
First to yawn,
Lookout Louie
Wakes at dawn
With his cat's
Pajamas on.

Eats his breakfast—
Juice and jam,
Triple-toasted
Cheese and ham—
Decides to send
An arrowgram.

Finds a feather,
Writes a poem,
Folds it neatly,
Sails it home.
Paper arrow
Hits the foam.

Lookout Louie
Hooks a star
With a string
From his guitar.
Sticky-Goo
Cannot be far.

Sticky-Goo at Last!

After *The Dog* had been tugged by the stars,
Louie gazed through yellow binoculars,
And saw a sea gull sign that said
ISLAND OF GOO—50 FEET AHEAD!
"Buns ahoy!" the First Mate roared,
Tossing the anchor overboard.

    Hail to The Dog *and the Fat-Cat crew!*
    Hail to the Queen of Catmandoo!
    Hail to me and hail to you!
    Sang Hillary Hollery Q. McQ.

The Mate did cartwheels. "Isn't this grand?!"
Wiggling his toes through the cinnamon sand.
From almond bushes and doughnut trees,
Icing ran down to the caramel seas.
The Captain, by means of a portable phone,
Cried, "Boys, leave the biscuits and bagels alone!
Fill up the barrels with buckets of Buns—
Rotten's in charge of the stickiest ones!"

Five Fat-Cats formed the Bun Brigade;
Stickies were carefully counted and weighed.
Up on the gangplank, down in the hold,
Rolled fourteen tons of the yeasty gold!
And H. H. Q., leaving nothing to chance,
Skewered a Bun with the tip of his lance.
As a bit of the Goo dribbled over his chin,
He puffed out his belly with a Captain's grin—

    What a wonderful Bun is a Sticky-Goo!
    If it sticks on me, it'll stick on you!
    Set the sails for Catmandoo!
    Sang Hillary Hollery Q. McQ.

ISLAND OF GOO 50 FEET AHEAD

Attack on the Poodles

Captain Captain had belly-flopped in for a dip
When Louie first spotted the enemy ship—
The Fifi—a Clipper of Poodles in pearls,
Sailing about with the wind in their curls.

Now Catty Moran always stood by his guns,
In case of attacks on the Sticky-Goo Buns.
His cannons, exploding with bubble bath powder,
Made *Fifi* keep barking, louder and louder.

He fired silk nightgowns, earrings, and lace—
The Poodles were drooling all over the place.
He hit them with bonbons and dark butter creams—
And, oh, what yip-yipping, what pitiful screams!

His taffy torpedoes (the saltwater kind)
Drove Chief Petty Poodle right out of her mind.
And after a blast of marshmallow harpoons,
The Poodles retreated, licking their wounds.

The battle was over before it began,
Thanks to the cannons of Catty Moran.
And he cried, "Now let that be a lesson to you!
A lesson no Poodle should *ever* pooh-pooh!"

An Octopus He and She

Not a fish would bite one windless night,
    Not a sound disturbed the crew
But the *plink-plink-plink*s of the tiddlywinks
    In the Captain's hobnailed shoe.

Then the pop-eyed Cook took a pop-eyed look
    At a beautiful sight at sea:
The courtship swoon by a buttermilk moon
    Of an Octopus he and she.

They kissed on the lips and the slithery hips,
    They kissed on the suction cups.
And they bobbed in the brine like a ball of twine
    Till at last the Lookout ups,

And he shouts, "Hey diddledy-dee for the squid!
    Hip-hip, hip-hip hurray!"
And arm in arm . . .
      in arm . . .
        in arm . . . ,
    The Octopi bobbed away.

On the Nowhere Isles

The Compass-Cat
Wore a porringer hat,
Which must have shrunk his brain,
For he set the dials
To the Nowhere Isles
In the thick of a thundering rain.

The weather soon cleared,
And the Fat-Cats cheered,
Nibbling on peppermint mice,
And the Captain fainted
At the rainbow painted
Over Nowhere Paradise.

Fat-Cats in boots
And bathing suits
Catnapped in the Nowhere sun.
The Cockatoos cooed
While the Cook shampooed
His whiskers one by one.

Flamingoes necked,
As you might expect,
And the Gunner assisted the Owl,
Who was helping a runt
On a wet truffle hunt
Dry them off with a paper towel.

We waved farewell
As coconuts fell
Out of Nowhere coconut trees.
And the Fat-Cats sang
To the animal gang
Somewhere on the Nowhere Seas!

The First Mate and the Whale Islands

Three blue whales went blubbering by,
Like islands on the sea.

Whistling a bit of a whaling tune,
A beautiful tune to me.

I scooped the bubbly, raised a toast—
"From Razor-Toes Jerome!"

We set the sails in the wake of the whales,
And followed those islands home.

The Return of The Frisky Dog

Out of the fog jumped *The Frisky Dog*,
    And it tickled my whiskered crew!
For we'd made it to port and the Royal Court
    Of the Queen of Catmandoo!

She sat on the dock with her eye on the clock,
    Wondering what had gone wrong,
And she said, "Dear Sir, would you kindly purr
    What has kept you at sea for so long?!"

Then she ate just one sweet Sticky-Goo Bun
    In delicate nibbles and bites,
And for our reward, she pulled out her sword
    And dubbed us the Fat-Cat Knights.

As I kissed her ring, she began to sing
    A ditty to the Fat-Cat crew,
A serenade for the Doo-Dah Parade
    Through the Hills of Catmandoo!
And all you could hear on this Happy New Year
    Was a *Meow* and a *Mew-mew-mew!*
      Dooby-dah, doo-dah-doo!
      A *Meow* and a *Mew-mew-mew!*

J. Patrick Lewis is the critically acclaimed author of picture books, both poetry and prose, for children. His first collaboration with Victoria Chess, *A Hippopotamusn't,* was universally praised, *Publishers Weekly* calling it "joyful exuberance...reminiscent of Ogden Nash." Other titles include *Two-Legged, Four-Legged, No-Legged Rhymes,* hailed as "one grand chorus of delight" by *The Horn Book,* and *The Moonbow of Mr. B. Bones,* a 1992 ALA Notable Book.

Mr. Lewis, the father of three, lives in Westerville, Ohio, and teaches at Otterbein College.

Victoria Chess is the deliciously wicked illustrator of *A Hippopotamusn't* by J. Patrick Lewis, *Spider Kane and the Mystery Under the May-Apple* and *Spider Kane and the Mystery at Jumbo Nightcrawler's,* both by Mary Pope Osborne, and *The Bigness Contest* and *Tales for the Perfect Child,* both by Florence Parry Heide.

Ms. Chess lives with her husband, two bull terriers, and two divine felines, Zazou and Pearl, in Connecticut.